Happy reading...
and voting!
Deborah

Peanut Butter or Jelly
A Story About Taking Turns (Or Not)

Story and Photographs by
Deborah Kelson

Dedicated to my (a)muse, Elliott Brown

First Printing
Printed in China

It was time for lunch. Peanut Butter and Jelly were spread on two slices of bread.

"Hey, Peanut Butter," said Jelly, "have you ever stopped to think why people call us *Peanut Butter and Jelly* and not *Jelly and Peanut Butter*?"

"Now that's a silly thought, Jelly," said Peanut Butter. "Why would anyone call us *Jelly and Peanut Butter*?"

"It's got a nice ring to it: *Jelly and Peanut Butter*. Maybe *my* name should go first in our sandwich," suggested Jelly.

"You mean, in *my* sandwich?" laughed Peanut Butter.

"My name comes first in the alphabet," proposed Jelly. "J comes six letters before P."

"Your name may come first in the alphabet, but my name has two words: Peanut and Butter. Two words are *twice* as many as one."

"I think we should focus on what's most important – taste!" exclaimed Jelly. "I'm sweet and last I checked, kids love sugar."

"Actually, many people prefer salty snacks to sweet ones. So that means I should still come first," explained Peanut Butter.

"Do you really think people like salt more than sugar, Peanut Butter? I'm beginning to think you are a CRAZY NUT!" snapped Jelly.

"Funny you bring that up!" chuckled Peanut Butter. "I'm actually not a nut. I'm a legume, which means I'm more like a seed than a nut."

"A legume, huh? I overheard a kid at the park talking about how much he loves legumes. **NOT**!" teased Jelly.

"At least I'm not the one who wets the bread," retorted Peanut Butter.

"What are you talking about?" whimpered Jelly.

Exhibit A

"While we're waiting around in the lunch box all morning, you soak through the bread and make a BIG MESS," accused Peanut Butter.

"Well... well, at least I don't get stuck to the roof of someone's mouth," argued Jelly.

"I've heard enough, my fructose-filled friend. This conversation is over. There is NO WAY anyone should call the sandwich *Jelly and Peanut Butter*," declared Peanut Butter.

"REALLY? You won't let me have a turn going first? Not even once?" pleaded Jelly.

"Nope.
Certainly not.
Absolutely not.
No way.
Nuh uh.
Not on your life.
No way, Jose.
Ixnay.
Negatory.
No dice.
No,"
negated
Peanut Butter.

"Well then, I guess this is how the story ends. I'm leaving," said Jelly. "Enjoy being all alone for the rest of your life in your boring *Peanut Butter and Nothing* sandwich."

"That's right.
IT'S MY SANDWICH!" shouted Peanut Butter.

"WAIT. WHAT?! You're leaving me? No! Please don't leave me," cried Peanut Butter. "I thought you would always stick around because you're... well, you're sticky."

INTRODUCING
JELLY AND
PEANUT BUTTER

"I'll stay under one condition: Change the name of the sandwich to *Jelly and Peanut Butter*," answered Jelly.

"Ugh. I really don't want to change our name. But let's work it out – for the sake of the children," replied Peanut Butter.

"I have an idea: Let's put it to a vote. Kids can decide what to call us," suggested Jelly.

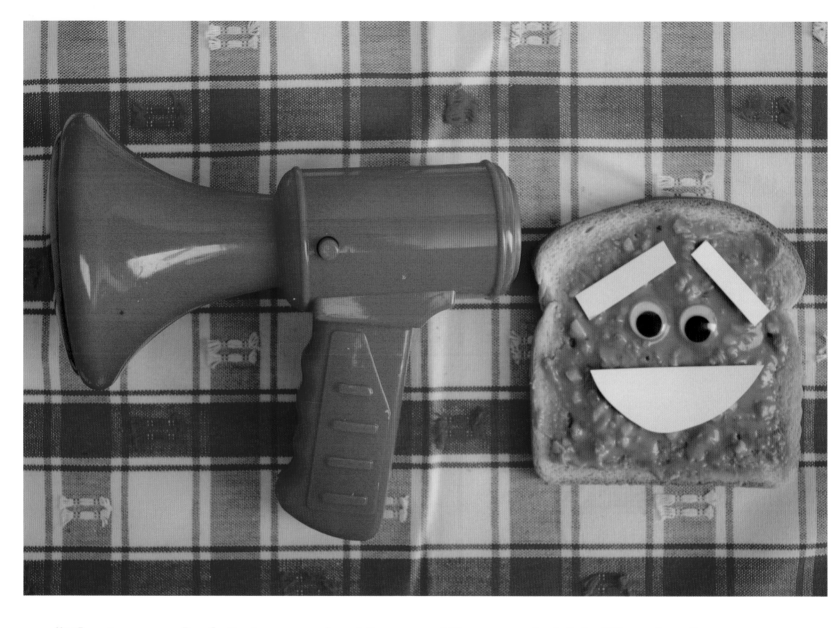

"That sounds fair to me, but how will we ask kids?" asked Peanut Butter. "We're just condiments. How are we going to *spread* the word?"

"Maybe a nice person will tell our story and create a website at
<u>www.peanutbutterorjelly.com</u> to track the votes," said Jelly.

"Well, I've always wanted my 15 minutes of fame. And until then, we're stuck together. So I'll see you between two slices of bread for lunch?" asked Peanut Butter.

"As long as the crusts are cut off," said Jelly, "I'll be there."

THE END

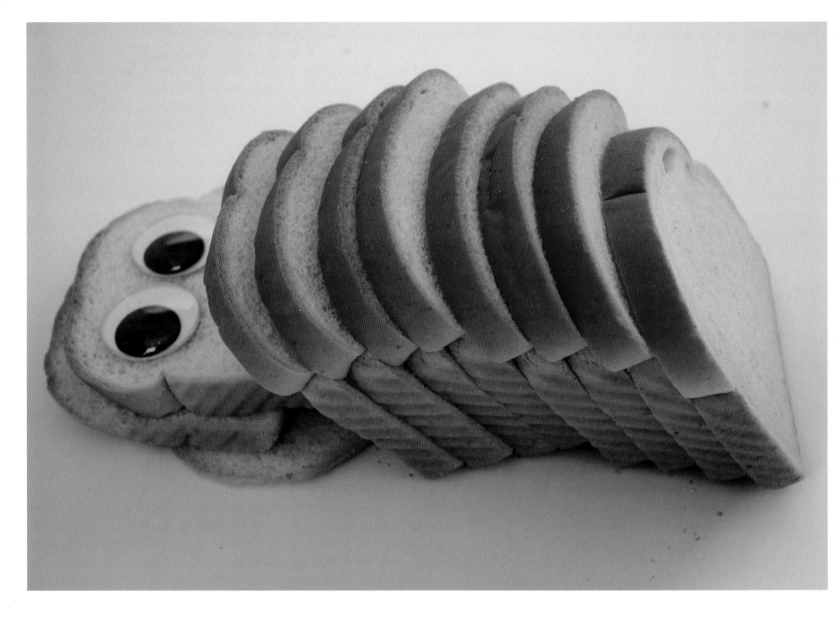

"Wait a second!" shouted Bread. "Why isn't my name in any sandwich? You know, there wouldn't be sandwiches without me. You could argue I'm the most important ingredient…"

THE END

For real this time.

Lunch is served.

Let your voice be heard.

Vote for *Peanut Butter and Jelly* or *Jelly and Peanut Butter.*

Vote for me and I'll be your best friend!

A vote for Jelly is a vote for change!

www.peanutbutterorjelly.com

You forgot me again! Consider Bread as your write-in candidate.